WELCOME TO THE

WYRD
WEST

GO BEYOND LEGEND

LEGENDS OF THE WYRD WEST

GHOST RIDERS

Bound by the spectres of an old frontier myth, a posse must defy the forces of the Law to do what is right and go beyond legend.

BROKEN WINGS

Erica's father suffers a manic fever to build a Flying Machine, but refuses to believe that a terrifying monster lurks below their ranch.

DREAD RECKONING

Royce Falco faces his last midnight in the haunted Hayworth Penitentiary before being sent to the gallows the next morning.

HORSE NATION

The Tobin brothers, investigating unexplained phenomena, become part of an Indian ceremony that they didn't know they were destined to join.

SILENT ECHOES

The only evidence of people vanishing from Echo Station are the telegraphed messages wired to Sundown, telling of sinister plague doctors.

WYRD WEST

DREAD RECKONING

L.T. PHOENIX

Dread Reckoning

Copyright © L.T. Phoenix 2021

Published by Phoenix Forge.

Print: ISBN: 9780994642653
Digital ISBN: 9780994642639

2.3

DREAD

RECKONING

"Any man's death diminishes me, because I am
involved in mankind. And therefore never send to
know for whom the bell tolls; it tolls for thee."

– John Donne
"Devotions Upon Emergent Occasions,
Meditation XVII"

XII

"That black cat is back again, crossing the road!" Michael McLaren couldn't believe his eyes. "Our tower shift almost over; so of course something weird happens."

"What, I'd hardly call that weird," the other guard on duty answered. "You sure it's the same one, Mick?"

"I dunno, cats all look the same to me. But it's black, and it keeps crossing the Road to Hell. You never use the spyglass..." McLaren handed the small sentry telescope over. "Use the spyglass!" He shook his head again. "This is bad luck, Reed... Bad luck, I tell ya."

"Well fugg me six ways from Sunday or my name ain't John Reed; that's gotta be the same cat." He wasn't as superstitious as the other, but shared his curiosity. "Why does it keep coming back? Just sits out there, then crosses the road, disappears when we're not looking, and comes back to cross the road again. And all in the cold like that with the night falling, to boot."

"And the storm clouds coming."

"Cats hate water; it's gonna get soaked," Reed agreed as he had an idea. "You know, I reckon that its master is probably inside."

"What, one of the prisoners? It's not a dog."

"Yeah, doesn't matter, it's probably pining for its master locked behind bars inside somewhere."

"Like I said, it's not a dog: it wouldn't do that."

"Why not?"

"I dunno, cat's just don't do that." McLaren braced his hands at the edge of the sentry tower, staring out at the cat as though it would bring him answers. "Poor creepy weird muttonhead. Just keeps staring at the prison."

"I bet you two bits, Mick," Reed reached inside his penitentiary uniform for the coins, "the cat is owned by one of the prisoners inside."

The other guard looked at the coins. "I'll take that bet, 'cos it's now up to you to ask some of that filth inside if they own a black cat and try to get a straight answer from any of them." McLaren laughed, adding, "Better start with Royce Falco and Clyde Mortimer; they won't be around after 5 o'clock tomorrow," while making a motion as though he was being choked by a noose.

"Don't remind me," Reed sighed. "I'm on death-watch tonight and execution in the morning. When the fugg are we supposed to sleep?"

"Me too, I'm with you for both. Hells teeth, who made the roster?" McLaren shivered. "I hate The Hole at night, and a black cat crossing the Road to Hell doesn't help things. The cells give me the creeps, and more guards have been seeing-

"Don't say it, Mick…"

A church bell rang across the prison, the sound so loud it hurt the ears.

"Hells bells… what was that?" McLaren looked around after the tolling was finished, not realising the irony of his cuss, having never heard such a bell toll in Hayworth Penitentiary.

"You just had to mention the hauntings, didn't you?" Reed searched around from the high view of the sentry tower, already sure he'd never find what could have made such a sound. "Is there a church and bell here now since my last shift?"

"I didn't say anything about the hauntings," McLaren argued, "but you did!"

"That wasn't the gallows bell, whatever it was; it's nowhere near as loud as that..." Reed spoke what they both already knew as a coping mechanism against the strange bell that was probably going to be thought of by all the guards of Hayworth Penitentiary as another haunting of The Hole. As much as he tried to reason the strange occurrence, it didn't help the unsettling feeling that began with the black cat continually crossing the aptly dubbed road that led into the prison and the effect both the animal and the mysterious bell tolling would have on them during the night shift. "So, why's this bell tolling, who's it for?"

"It sounded like a passing bell, you know, rings like that from a church before someone... dies... There's no executions at sundown to be tolled for," McLaren added, "only the two at five o'clock in the morning for Mortimer and Falco..."

XI

The loud tolling of the unusual bell throughout the prison had unsettled guards and inmates of Hayworth Penitentiary.

All except for Clyde Mortimer. The old man found the subduing effect it had on everybody amusing.

As Royce Falco was led to the cell that he would spend his last night in, marched by guards beside the other prisoner considered by most to be a lunatic, a rat crossed their path.

Mortimer jumped from his guard's loose grip, possessing an uncanny agility despite his age and the shackles binding his wrists. With limbs like spindles, he stomped after the rat.

"Mortimer! Get back here or I'll knock you senseless again," one of the guards threatened.

Royce, as shackled as Clyde, wriggled free from his own guard's hold in the commotion and shoulder-rushed the cruel old man against some cell bars. But, to Royce's dismay, it wasn't before Clyde had managed to injure the rat, the creature squealing and limping away.

"Aww," Mortimer began, a mock face of sympathy, "did the little rat getting hurt upset the *infamous* Royce Falco?"

"If you men weren't already hanging tomorrow, I'd beat you to pulp!" Royce's guard went to reclaim his prisoner.

Royce evaded, dodging. Then with his eyes set squarely on Mortimer, he launched at the lunatic. Royce's forehead hit the front of the other's skull with such force that the back of the old man's head struck the bars of their new cells.

Clyde Mortimer just laughed as Royce's guard finally managed to grab him and keep him from attacking further. "Royce Falco, *Red Roy*, *Famous Rat Lover of The Hole*. They should call you Rat Roy instead!" His laughter became maniacal as the other guard brought him to his feet and told him to, "Shut the fugg up."

Falco and Mortimer were put in separate cells beside each other. These spaces were to be where they would contemplate their last hours before being hanged to death by noose the next morning.

As Mortimer's guard exited the area with the other, he said without much sympathy, "God be with you..."

Mortimer snorted. It was one of the strangest responses Royce had ever heard from the crazed man as he himself pondered the absurdness of the guard's sentiment.

Mortimer rubbed his bleeding head to see how much blood he could squeeze in his fingers. "You gonna say one of them little *Injun* prayers for the rat, Red Roy?"

"Fugg off, Mortimer, don't call me that."

"Awww, come on... Rat Roy... Alright... Royce... Say one for me."

"I wouldn't fugging waste my breath on you, that's for damned sure."

"But the guard said *God be with you* to me..." Mortimer sat with his legs huddled in his arms. "I must *deserve* a prayer."

"*God be with you?* What does that even mean to people before the gallows?" Royce looked to Mortimer, seeing the pathetic old man playing with the blood from his head wounds like a child. "You deserve nothing but the noose. You can wait for a preacher, I ain't saying fugging nothing for you. The rat deserves a prayer more than you, the poor forsaken thing, after what you damn well did to it. But not you. Never you."

"But it's just vermin, Royce."

"No, Clyde, you're vermin. That rat had more class in just its tail than you have in your whole wrinkled body."

"And they say I'm crazy? Why would you pray for a filthy rodent and not the man across your cell going to the gallows with you?"

"I dunno." Royce nonchalantly replied, rubbing his forehead where he had struck Mortimer. "Probably just another bad habit I picked up from one of my brothers."

"Fugg!" Reed dropped his bits, the coins falling through the wood floorboards of the sentry tower. "Where'd he come from?"

McLaren raised the spyglass to see. "When did he get there?"

The cat never removed itself from the area. It switched at random moments between a staunch vigil staring at the front of Hayworth Penitentiary and making unnerving crossings of the road that led into the prison, despite the great tolling of the mysterious church bell.

At some point the cat was doing neither activity, instead having its black coat scratched by the white-gloved hand of a stranger in blue.

"That's what I'm saying!"

"Yeah," McLaren said, "but I didn't see him approach."

"Neither the fugg did I." Reed explained again. "That's what I'm talking about."

"Did he just sneak up?"

"Well, where from?"

Hayworth Penitentiary, located a safe and civilised distance outside La Grande, was situated in a large valley within a high hill. A Wakoda legend told that the formation was caused by a fire that fell from the sky to the earth. This garnered the penitentiary and the hill what some considered to be a misnomer; *The Hole*, as it is known among the prisoners and workers. From the sentry tower, anyone ascending the rise over the hill and descending into the valley toward the prison should be spotted with ease a literal mile away.

And the road that led into the prison under the sentry tower was known across the territory as the Road to Hell. There was a small weathered sign almost out of sight from the sentry tower beside the road that McLaren had put up years earlier, that the Warden hadn't had removed because of the reputation it garnered the prison among criminals. The branded letters read by anyone approaching the penitentiary and often recited out loud by prisoner wagon guards to their passengers bound for incarceration:

Last Road into Hell.

The man had kneeled to the cat, but not enough to put the crisp midnight-blue trousers to the cobbled road leading into Hayworth Penitentiary. As he scratched the animal under the chin, it looked as though he spoke to it.

The stranger stood, pulling a pocket watch from his vest, checking it with a refined posture. Closing it, he stepped toward the prison entrance, the black cat remaining in place despite the approaching storm.

"We'd better alert the gate, Mick, that we have an incoming visitor," Reed stated.

McLaren looked at the sentry tower's old timepiece as some guards approached. "Ah, good. Our shift's almost up, and here comes the tower night shift. We'll just go down to the gate ourselves on our way to death-watch. I wanna know who walks alone all the way along the Road to Hell when a black cat keeps crossing it during an approaching storm!"

IX

"But, what you must ask yourselves, good sirs, is this…" There was a hanging pause as the distinguished accent drifted through the barren cell corridor like a gentle breeze. "Was the card you chose at the beginning of this simple prestidigitation really the card you had chosen at all?"

Royce heard the guards' exclamation of astonishment; he could even feel their sense of questioning awe from inside his cell.

"You got a visitor, Falco," McLaren called down the hall, then added with a humoured tone of disbelief, "says he's your *preacher.*"

John Reed and Michael McLaren's curiosity about the approaching stranger paid off when they were treated to card tricks beyond belief, so much so that they agreed to escort him to see a prisoner in the exact location of where their next shift was. It was happenstance that defied convenience, McLaren chalked it up to good fortune.

Mortimer chuckled from his cell, next to Royce's. "The rat's family have come to send you straight to Hell!"

Royce's brow clenched. "That doesn't even make sense; you're the one that was cruel to it."

"Life," Mortimer screamed into his pillow, "doesn't make sense."

Royce had an idea of who was coming; someone that hadn't appeared in his life for some years. As soon as the distinguished gentleman walked in to view there was no doubt to the answer of Mortimer's question of, "Who's this, dandy?"

Royce answered. "Charles Lafayette..."

The visitor raised a finger to the brim of his wide hat as an interjection. "The One and Only, Charles Lafayette, Legendary Mysterio, Illusionist, Magician, Perceptivist, Master of Cosmology, Esoterica, Fortuna, Portentia and Mysticism..." He pulled on the brim of his hat as he gave a slight bow of acknowledgement to Mortimer.

"That's a lotta fugging turd words, mister."

"Charming..." Lafayette turned to face the other prisoner.

Royce smirked. "So, how did you work your way into the restricted area that the guards call death-watch?"

"Simple tricks," the magician nodded his head back at Mortimer, "appease the simplest of minds."

"I'll fugg you up," Mortimer tried to rattle the bars of his cell, "you dandy Creole!"

Lafayette returned to the wiry old man, twirling his moustache with thought, his azure gaze piercing. "Execution at the noose is too simple of an escape for the sins you have committed, Clyde Mortimer, but there's a special place after the gallows where there is no escaping from what you did to that little girl at Rosewood..."

Royce couldn't believe it. He'd never seen Mortimer shut down like that. The man was without remorse, and no amount of reasoning could ever silence him. Only beatings by guards to the point of unconsciousness had any effect. Lafayette had somehow plucked just the right thread to unravel the lunatic, Mortimer weaking at the knees to almost fall to the floor, his wrinkled skin looking as though he'd spent a night out in the cold.

Lafayette came back to Royce's cell, those azure eyes gazing through the vertical bars at the prisoner. The man once known as Red Roy didn't know what to make of the magician's visit, but he knew such an appointment was never to be taken lightly. Royce didn't know what to say, but tried, "It's been a while, Chu-"

Royce paused as the magician's brow raised, rethinking his naming, "-arles..."

Charles Lafayette nodded, Royce seeing a small, satisfied smile across his lips. Then the magician delivered mysterious words in the manner he was known for – by the few that did know him well enough for that.

"This is where it all ends. As the evening passes and a storm of liberation descends upon Hayworth Penitentiary, you, Royce Falco, will face your Last Midnight."

Royce swallowed. "Grim tidings, Lafayette."

"Indeed." The magician continued. "You will also confront your brothers and your last chance at redemption. One of these brothers, in particular, has seen to it that your execution is scheduled alongside *this*"- he was referring to Mortimer - "so that it may go unnoticed by your father of whom you are used to delivering your salvation against the Law."

"Kayne..." Royce knew it.

"The very same." Lafayette acknowledged. "The man that would be king among the Falco dynasty. Kayne Falco, he who vies with you for the coveted position as the Seventh Son of a Seventh Son."

"So why don't you use one of your magic tricks to spring me from this prison so Kayne doesn't get his way?"

"Your Doom is upon you, Royce Falco," Lafayette explained. "All the powers of the universe move in cohesion so that you face the reckoning of one Last Midnight. You must choose redemption or death as your Fate."

"Then I choose redemption! As if I'd choose anything else..."

"Redemption, my dear Royce, isn't simply a matter of uttering a succession of traditional words – no, not at all, that won't do, that form of tyranny just will not do. You'll need to tell *them* of your decision and mean it, because they can see right through any deceit."

"Who... Tell who?" Royce was wary.

"You'll know when the time is upon you. There's many who still linger beyond death in Hayworth Penitentiary, and *they* are coming tonight..."

VIII

Royce woke with the feeling that there was a weight upon his chest and that something was watching him.

He had spent years in the wilds of the West, becoming accustomed to being prepared against predatory animals and raiders. Such was his life when he abandoned the Falco family, adopting the ways of an outlaw constantly on the fringes of civilisation and running from the Law.

He opened his eyes at a gradual pace; the ploy being that one could hopefully peer through their eyelids without an assailant detecting that their target was awake. Even with all that knack learned surviving the harsh frontier of the West, Royce wasn't prepared for what he saw.

A nightmarish beast clutched a limp rat in its jaws above his face, Royce bolting upright with fright as his heart pounded at the sight.

It had already been difficult enough for Royce to fall asleep in a prison that was said to be haunted, even with a belly swollen with his Last Meal. But he also had to contend with the murderous madman in the next cell that slept his meal off like a child without a worry in the world - and he snored like a wayward ship blowing a foghorn in the darkest of nights. The impending dread that death was upon them in the morning didn't grip Mortimer as it had Royce.

Startled, he had catapulted the weight of a black cat from his chest – immediately apologetic! - to the hard floor at the foot of his bed.

"Memphis! Memphis...?" Royce recognised the feline. "What the fugg are you doing here...? Where's Lafayette?"

The rat had managed to stay clamped in the cat's face that had become a picture of rejection. Lafayette's pet spat the creature, releasing it, as Royce recognised the rodent from the fracas earlier. The rat hobbled away toward Mortimer's cell, still showing signs of its injury.

"Oh no, don't go near him!"

Dark clouds blocked what little moonlight sifted in through the bars of the small cell window. But with the faint glow of lantern light from the death-watch station around the corridor corner and eyes adjusted to darkness, Royce was able to quickly scoop the limping creature into his hands. He knew he had probably saved it from suffering a fate worse than the one it had scarcely escaped from earlier if Mortimer had woken.

Under Memphis' watchful gaze, Royce wrapped the rat in part of the foot-end of his blanket to create a little nest. His bed was only a wooden ledge, supported by two chains from a rough wall, but it was all he could provide. While the blanket was of poor quality, the rodent showed no protest to the act of kindness and the feline didn't appear to have any further interest in the other creature. It seemed that Memphis had brought the rat as an odd gift. Although, if Royce thought about it long enough, he knew this would somehow relate to some sort of peculiar exploit of Charles Lafayette.

Royce bent a side of his pillow up, revealing leftover scraps he'd smuggled away from his Last Meal.

After being told he couldn't have veal or a duck carcass, Mortimer had requested that he only wanted beef - still on the bone - and a bottle of Thirsty Mule whisky. Both meals had come with mashed potatoes topped with butter and gravy alongside steamed beans, carrots and corn.

Royce had declined meat when asked, wanting only to eat plants and drink tea. He saw no point in needlessly taking another life from the world when his own life wasn't going to continue. His indulgence was some gingerbread and rock candy.

After hearing Royce ask for it, Mortimer had added the same treats to his order like a child experiencing the fear of missing out. That was the second time he had seen the old lunatic fearful, a feeling that Royce previously didn't think Mortimer was capable of experiencing, the first being when Lafayette informed him that death would be no escape from punishment for the terrible crimes he had committed in life.

The Warden of Hayworth Penitentiary, Harry Linch, had made his presence known when the meals were delivered to the death-watch cells. He was a curious man that wore a monocle and carried a walking cane despite not needing either, strolling with the grace of La Grande's high society that he belonged to – a grace that was wasted within these dirty halls that stank of impending death where none of that pageantry mattered. His visit wasn't to introduce himself, nor was it to offer any sympathies, it was simply to appear magnanimous alongside the Last Meals. He presented himself as though he had graciously produced these final pleasures intended for the wicked with his own hands –

but really, it just seemed to be an encounter of repetition, of pre-execution ritual.

Harry Linch did perform one unexpected duty; denying Clyde Mortimer a rather visceral conjugal request that involved the Warden's entire family – the Warden included! Whilst that request would upset the stomachs of most, it only increased the appetite of the lunatic murderer.

Royce had hidden some of his meal to help him get through the night, to pass the time - what little of it remained - if getting to sleep was going to be difficult.

He held a piece of loose corn, that he had stripped from the cob earlier, near the rat's nose. "I don't know if this is any good for you," Royce whispered, "but do you want it?" The creature took the offering in both forepaws, its nose and whiskers twitching, and nibbled on the yellow food.

Royce watched the rat. "Corn, hey?" He offered the creature another piece. "Every soul deserves a name. You will be... *corn*... Cornelius."

"And what about you?" Royce held an offering to the cat, knowing very well that Memphis was unlikely to accept anything. "Carrot?" Memphis was as disinterested in the vegetable as a cat could possibly be.

The snoring had stopped and the old lunatic started, "Looks like somebody else's *conjiggle* request was approved." Mortimer chuckled, slapping his knee. "A rat in your bed. You really are a Rat Lover."

After laughing louder, the wrinkled man answered, "And no, Roy, you can stick your fugging carrot where the sun don't shine."

"Shut up, Mortimer," Royce still spoke softly, not wanting to attract attention from the guards. He realised that Memphis was nowhere to be seen and hadn't been spotted by Mortimer, which was bizarre as there was no simple escape route - it was, however, Lafayette's mysterious black cat, so Royce knew to expect no less.

"I bet your *Injun* name would be, *Sleeps with Rats*." The lunatic guffawed.

McLaren called from the death-watch station, "Shut the fugg up Mortimer!"

"But," Mortimer was to the bars of his cell, "there's a rat in here!"

Royce went over to the other cell and reached through to Mortimer's arm. He yanked the madman against their shared bars, the head-wound reopening. "Close. Your. Mouth."

As Reed made his way into the cell corridor, answering, "I know, Mortimer, you're it, and I'll give you a drubbing like the rat you are," Royce was already back in his cot, stashed food and a nestled rat covered as though nothing was amiss.

Mortimer cussed, "Fugg you!" He sat back on his own wooden ledge. "Roy's got a rat. Give it to me, I'll get rid of it."

"Last time, Mortimer," the guard warned.

"Chew the meat off the bones," the old man imitated the motions, "slurp the blood from the tail like the nectar of a dead harlot."

Reed beat his baton along Mortimer's cell bars while reaching for keys. The lunatic rolled back and drew his blanket over himself, not wanting to be beaten back to sleep. The guard waited a few seconds to see if there was another peep, then returned to his station.

While the rat was warm in its nest, the cat was still nowhere to be seen.

In the seconds after Reed had left, Royce could see through his almost-closed eyes that a locomotive engineer was standing outside the cells. He wore all the clothing and trappings one could expect of a train driver; overalls, gloves, the cap. The face drew his attention the most, as though he could recall it from the past. The most disturbing part was that Royce could see through him to the wall on the other side...

He didn't startle as he had when the cat was upon him, the years of preparedness still held true for most things – even if not a magician's cat.

"That'd be right," Royce muttered, almost so the apparition could hear him, "I'm sharing my Last Midnight with a murdering lunatic and a fugging ghost who's face I can't recall."

Like Mortimer, he rolled over to face his wall and shut his eyes, being careful that his feet didn't disturb the wounded rat. "You're alright, Cornelius, but I don't have time for this other fuggunshyt."

All Royce could do was force himself back to sleep.

VII

Royce Falco awoke again, this time to the unmistakable gentle rocking of a moving train. After the incident with Memphis delivering a rat, he was mentally prepared for whatever imagery could assault his senses next.

The soothing sway of train car travel had come first, followed by the sibilance of released steam pressure. Then the low mechanical squeal of metal upon metal as big wheels turned upon their tracks. Dim voices murmured their conversations all around as a newspaper rustled. Through the wary slits of those vigilant eyes, he was greeted by some of the great green plains of Wakoda Territory passing by outside the glass of his train car window.

Royce sat up from his restful slump, moving strands of hair from his face, and realised that there was a hat upon his head.

Charles Lafayette sat across the aisle from him in their facing chairs, engrossed in a thin book with a gilded title, *Rime of the Ancient Mariner*. A pair of children ran between them, one wielding what could only be described as a wooden executioner's axe and the other pulling a raggedy doll along by a twine noose around its neck. A man in another chair along the car read a newspaper with a very bold headline, *Wanted for Mass Murder: Royce "Red Roy" Falco*. Somewhere else in the carriage a group of women argued about how it was possible for the Messiah to rise from the dead.

"What the fugg?" Royce bolted straight. "Did you bust me out of The Hole?"

"Not at all, dear Royce. I explained that I wouldn't partake of such mediocrity. A phenomenal feat of escapology from Hayworth Penitentiary, worthy of the ages, will be of your own reckoning."

Royce felt something wiggle in his leg pocket.

Further to his surprise that he was wearing a hat, he wasn't wearing the black and white bee-stripes that Hayworth Penitentiary issued their prisoners. Instead, he was decked in the garb of his days living the frontier life; his favourite bowler hat, red kerchief, jacket, trousers with chaps and boots. Assuredly, he knew it was his attire as there were no spurs on the boots – never spurs, Royce hated the idea of them. Although he did feel slightly naked without a holstered revolver hanging from his side.

He reached into the wriggling pocket, producing the injured rat that he had comforted in the blanket of his prison cot.

"What's this?" Royce held the sniffing creature before the magician.

"One would be forgiven for thinking it to be simply a common brown rat," Lafayette answered, twirling his moustache, "although I do believe that his appellation is *Cornelius*." The magician considered the creature with a fondness not usually offered to rats. "Although the probability is that he is the runt of the litter, he remains a handsome fellow. Fortune favoured this creature after his encounter with Clyde Mortimer, Fate having brought you and Cornelius together."

"Are you done? I know what a rat is." Of course, Royce thought, Lafayette somehow knew the name given to the rat – and there'd probably be no point asking how or why. "What's Cornelius doing here... did you bring him to the prison?" He looked around the train, looking for some sign that this experience wasn't real. "Are we even still in Hayworth?"

"Why is Cornelius here, you ask? You are the merciful one whom always takes pity upon unfortunate creatures and decided no differently with this unique specimen. Your strands of Fate have crossed paths. A question, if you will: why did you hide Cornelius from pitiless eyes and nourish him with rations that you secreted away for yourself after Mortimer's cruelty?"

"Because they're always better with me."

"They...?"

"Animals. They're always better with me."

"They are always better *with* you... or, are they always better *because* of you?"

"It's hard to say."

"Is it really so difficult, Royce?"

"Fine. Fugg." Royce shrugged. "Animals in my care always seem to get better, heal, become healthy. Sometimes, even people. It just happens. I don't get it. I don't know why."

"But of course, you do, dear Royce. Those that you choose to take under your protective vigilance benefit from your more... *miraculous*... qualities. You know what occurs, you simply don't acknowledge that it is anything as extraordinary as it really is."

There was a pause as Royce and Lafayette's eyes engaged across the train car aisle over a truth given form by speaking of it out loud.

The magician added, "You are the Seventh Son of a Seventh Son - a familial position,

Royce, that you have struggled to reckon with for all your life - such power is your domain."

"What if I'm not the Seventh... Kayne, he could easily be the Seventh - we were born on the same day. We have the same father, but only because our *beloved* Papa forced himself upon the mother I never knew while on one of his fugged-up crusades across the West. I bleed half my father's Falco blood and half my mother's Wakoda blood. I am less Falco than Kayne, he's whole – he's *pure*, as the family likes to say - and I felt more kinship with my one Wakoda brother than any of my Falco brothers."

"Fate has graced these gifts upon you whether you feel destined to have them or not." Lafayette took on a look of concern. "I am glad that you have spoken fondly of your Wakoda brother, for I bring good tidings that he has accepted the Fate that he once refused..."

"Hawk?"

"The very same, although he has returned to a name that he had not held dear for some time."

"Red Hawk?"

"Almost..."

"No, not..." Royce could see the understanding in Lafayette's piercing blue eyes. "You mean..."

Lafayette's raised brow lingered for Royce's response.

"*Thunder Hawk...?*"

"Indeed. Thunder Hawk, the Wakoda Spiritwalker has returned." The magician was pleased with Royce's deduction. "Your good brother has forged new alliances during your absence beyond the single company of the irritable veteran, and has passed your Aetron to one of them."

"Well," Royce remembered, "I never expected to see my Aetron pendant - or Hawk - again."

Lafayette continued. "What you must understand is that Fate brought them together. Your brother was Doomed by his own misguided actions, but this new partnership, this band of outlaws as they have become, they altered his Fate by defying the Law and embracing an old frontier legend."

"Sounds like something Hawk would do. He'd take on the Law if he's a Spiritwalker again."

"Whilst he is a Spiritwalker, their plight against the Law is far from over and will eventually bring them against those more powerful in the Falco dynasty. In this regard, they are without direction."

Royce released a silent sigh. "Why are you telling me this?"

"Dear Royce, you must take them under that same protective vigilance that you show more to animals than people. You must guide them through the tribulations to come – not around, but through - the only way around is through…"

"How am I supposed to do that when I'm stuck in some…" Royce thought a moment… "dream train… that may as well be headed toward the gallows?"

"The answer to that question is why you are here aboard, but this is no dream train." The magician waved his hand across the view of the endless plains. "Depending on your perception, you are either: residing in Hayworth Penitentiary as a prisoner of your own mind, or you are travelling as a passenger aboard a vehicle of the landscapes of your own conscience."

Royce's mouth opened, but he didn't know what words to use.

In response, Lafayette explained. "This train carries neither the blessed nor the damned. These souls are each at the very edge of a personal reckoning that will decide their Fate. Whilst this train travels through a realm of Mysterium, it is destined to arrive shortly at one of three points of Fate in your own history that contributed to you being wanted across Wakoda Territory as the outlaw, Red Roy."

"What three, Chuck? What do you mean?"

Lafayette's eyes widened at the use of the nickname, *Chuck.*

Royce was becoming thoroughly confused. "Does Kumiko still hang out with you? Can we get her to translate your babble?"

"Miss Watanabe," the magician's wide brim hat lowered, covering his eyes, "is no longer in my employ as a Magician's Assistant."

"Dang." Royce crossed his arms with disappointment. "Did she get sick of your cryptic shenanigans?"

"Somewhat, to that end..." Lafayette answered with pause. "Miss Watanabe chose to diverge from the Fate I had seen for her."

"We can do that? So then, what are these three Fates you have seen for me?"

"Dear Royce, I ask you, to which incidents of your life are you the most confident of being in the moral right rather than the lawful right?"

"Well, I don't know which three would be the best three – there's a helluva lot of times the Law didn't agree with my point of view of what's right and what's wrong."

"The first," Lafayette explained, "was the incident at Miss Kitty's in Sundown. You killed all the men attempting to have their way with a lady of the night against her will. The only man you left alive that evening was a patron that was passing by that did nothing for the lady despite her pleas. Thus, in response, you hung him from Miss Kitty's balcony by his ankles, upside down, as naked as the day he was born, for all of Sundown to see his shame."

"The Law may not have been pleased," Royce chuckled to himself, smiling, "but Miss Kitty was."

"Another, in Mudflats, you broke up a dog-fighting ring, killing all the trainers and almost everyone there who had placed a wager. You freed all the healthy animals, managed to escape in a wagon with all the injured canines and their newly-born offspring. You even, afterward, then rescued from a vengeful parent, one of the healthy dogs that had bitten their child."

"That mutt didn't know any better - it had been raised that way. And I wasn't going to let the pups of fighting dogs be murdered either - Buddy was one of them, who you know, so you know that they can be raised better..." Royce gazed longingly into the past. "I wish I could see that red furball just one last time."

"And, somewhere between the train stations of Echo and Sundown you-

"That's the one," Royce decided, "the buffalo hunting train!"

"Indeed," Lafayette raised an eyebrow.

"Yup." Royce nodded. "How about, instead, I tell you how that one went down."

"There will be no need..."

"What? Why?"

"Because we are already arriving at that moment in time..."

"So we just arrive at it... there... in the past?"

"Yes, precisely."

"Fugging madness, but giddy-up!"

"Indeed."

Royce stood with confidence. "This was where I was the most justified I've ever been."

"Excellent, show me what led to that..."

"I will. Can't wait."

"Thus it shall be..."

VI

Royce was woken by a crack of thunder as the storm outside grew stronger. Waking, it seemed, had become the trend of this dreaded night.

The train dream hadn't appeared to have led anywhere, and he was wearing the horizontal prison stripes again. Usually when Lafayette laid the heavy language on with enigmatic statements like, *thus it shall be*, bizarre twists of fortune followed.

But, perhaps it was simply a dream?

Staring out of the small barred window of Royce's cell was a bearded man also wearing the stripes of Hayworth Penitentiary. A noose hung from his neck, the rope's cut end not swaying despite the chill damp gusts of the increasing storm. There was a soft glow about him that

mixed with what little moonlight was available –
moonlight that cast no shadow.

Royce, with little care in his voice, joked to
the... to... *it*, "Is there somewhere else you need
to be, or are you just gonna *hang* around for a
while?"

The spectre didn't react. It continued to
peer out of those bars as though it longed for
some touch of freedom it could never have.

If it wasn't the spirit of a train driver, it
was the ghost of a prisoner. Royce was as
comfortable as one could be with most
occurrences like this; he'd seen his share and
often was told by the Falco family and its
associates that the gift was the province of the
Seventh Son. The only times he wasn't
comfortable with such visions was when they
were malevolent – it was during those moments
that Royce took exception to the supernatural.

It still hadn't passed the stroke of midnight.

Many destined for the gallows would wish
for time to slow down or even stand still to
avoid their impending demise. Royce's Last
Midnight was taking forever. Unless Lafayette's
visitations were going to give him some meaning
or insight against this dilemma, he simply wished
the inevitable Last Midnight would pass and the
sun would dawn upon the end of his life at the
end of a rope.

The injured rat was still resting at the end of the bed under the blanket, the little covered sanctuary having become quite warm. "Cornelius, why didn't I ask Lafayette about that fugging weird bell tolling while I had the chance?" The rat made a chattering sound in response. "All I did was ask about Kumiko."

As if the unasked question of Lafayette tapped into a well of mysteriousness, Royce felt a strange shift in the atmosphere. There was an uncomfortable feeling in the air coming from the death-watch station.

It wasn't the ghost staring at the storm that had truly started to beat down before he woke up with the rain, cold, thunderbolts and flashes of light flickering through barred windows. It was that a disturbance had presented itself nearby, something sinister had made itself known.

The spectre had vanished while out of sight when McLaren and Reed led three strangers into the cell corridors.

You wouldn't know if they were man or woman, cloaked in heavy flowing black robes. Under a straight-brimmed black hat, each wore the most unsettling mask. Dark-lensed goggles covered the eyes of the mask while a pointed black leather snout – shaped like a raven's beak - protruded from the mouth.

Royce had seen a number of different spook hats in his years, but none were ever as intricately strange or disconcerting as these. Many of them had appeared among clandestine gatherings at the Falco mansion when he was growing up, their wearers often holding great interest in Royce and his brother, Kayne.

They possessed the blessing to do their will by the rich and powerful and given autonomy to override law enforcement by the government - and it is said in quiet corners of the West that they dabble in occult magic. From their reputations gained centuries prior against the Black Death and other plagues of Europe and the British Isles, their function was to investigate, control and cure disease.

They were known as plague doctors. They ventured where only rats dared go, followed the sick, and enacted their reputably divine purpose wherever they appeared.

Royce found himself standing, staring at one of the three as he... or she... it... stared back.

McLaren and Reed unlocked Mortimer's cell, went in and woke the snoring madman.

"What?" Mortimer panicked, seeing the thundering conditions outside through his own little square barred window. "I wasn't making any noise – it was the fugging weather!"

"Here he is: Clyde Mortimer," Reed presented.

McLaren added, "Facing the gallows for murdering perhaps more than a hundred men and women from Alabaster to Rosewood."

Mortimer chuckled. "You're leaving out all the interesting details, they weren't all men and women – animals, fish, children..."

"The gruesome details, you mean, you sick fugger." Reed slapped Clyde upside his head "We don't want to know."

"These visitors need to examine you before your execution," McLaren explained.

"Examinations?" Mortimer's annoyance of being awoken was soon replaced by vile impulses. "I like examinations." He looked to each plague doctor, suddenly compliant. "I like to take turns."

Royce's spine shivered at Mortimer's words before he spoke to the goggles of the beaked mask that remained pointed his way. "Do I know you?"

The plague doctor didn't flinch.

As the guards led Mortimer from his cell and headed toward the death-watch station, the old lunatic asked the plague doctors in tow, "Tell me, in your examinations, have any of you ever had the pleasure of sticking a man's head on a spike?"

Just before Royce's plague doctor exited the corridor, he tried one last time to get a response. "Kayne *Septimus* Falco."

The plague doctor flinched, pausing in its next step for a second, before continuing around the corner as though nothing was amiss.

Royce grunted, getting nothing of worth. He doubted it, but perhaps the plague doctor could at least be useful by not bringing Mortimer back.

"Look out, Cornelius." He fell to his bed, the thin padding and wood of the ledge a little hard for comfort, hands running through his hair. "Fugginell, what's going on around here? I've seen some weird shyt before, but this place wins a prize. Fugging Mortimer. Fugging plague doctors... here?"

As thunder rumbled outside, Royce closed his eyes, trying not to think about the shadowy physicians. Instead, he tried to imagine why Lafayette wanted him involved with his Wakoda brother and the new posse of outlaws he rode with.

It was impossible: he faced the noose on his next morning. It was living the life of an outlaw that saw his neck headed toward the end of that executioner's rope time and again. What good could come from continuing that trend?

It's a nice dream, Royce thought, but Lafayette's musings couldn't outweigh the encompassing dread that continued to gnaw at the inevitable reality that nothing mattered any more as his life was going to end.

Unlike times before when he'd faced execution, this time there didn't appear to be an escape from his inevitable Doom.

61

"Finally!" The unfamiliar young man's voice broke through the haze in Royce's head. "We've got ourselves a herd of buffalo for the killing!"

It had taken him some time to force himself to sleep again after the intrusion of the plague doctors and his dwelling thoughts upon his hopeless mortality. Royce didn't care for the lunatic, but he was also troubled that Clyde Mortimer hadn't been returned to his cell. And he was left with the nagging question of whether his brother, Kayne, had anything to do with the black-clad strangers.

When Royce Falco was awoken by the youthful guffawed announcement of a buffalo sighting, he was in a different train car seat to the one he and the magician had been aboard earlier, feeling a different rocking sensation as he regained consciousness. And this time, Lafayette was nowhere to be seen.

Royce was wearing the frontier attire he had in the previous... dreamscape - was it a dream? Is this a dream, are these scenes actually elaborate artifices of Lafayette, or a symptom of the mind caused by knowing that your impending Doom draws ever nearer?

Cornelius was in his pocket again – or in his pocket still, depending upon how Royce thought about it - remaining calm and enjoying the warmth.

He recognised the train he was onboard: it really was the third choice Lafayette had proffered. The difference in the current moment to that of the past was that he had approached this particular train on a champion of a horse that he had named Meteor, and gained entry via the caboose.

Men of all ilk responded to the news of buffalo sighted by raising the windows of the passenger car and pointing their weapons outside. The train slowed, attempting to match their targets' speed.

This was one of the many railroads and trains owned by Royce's father, the German railroader, Oskar Falco. The industrialist had seen fit to advertise specifically endorsed *Buffalo Hunting by Railroad* on train lines that were especially prone to damage from bison on the tracks. This sort of commercially sanctioned slaughter attracted the likes of government agents, professional hunters, fur traders, trophy collectors and other men from all walks of life. They were young and old, some simply in it for the thrill of the kill.

It also bettered Oskar Falco's interests that the U.S. Army endorsed this sort of carnage to diminish the plains Indian's primary means of survival, something his military ally, Captain Phileas Cordell, enjoyed. This degree of mass slaughter forced the native populations away from the railroads. Tycoons like the Gold Baroness of Wakoda Territory, Twyla Matthias, had also poured funds into supporting the massacre of buffalo in a bid to take more land away from the Indians.

A herd of bison, commonly called buffalo, had begun to stampede away from the train, but still ran mostly alongside it.

The train's matching speed was perfect as its passengers eagerly opened fire, plumes of white blossoming to release faint whiffs of gunpowder. Men had shouldered to the gangways between cars to set up positions for shooting. Others had clambered onto the rooves for a clearer vantage point. An open-topped boxcar with barely any freight – a deliberate decision for railroad buffalo hunting – was continuing to fill with shooters looking to make their kills.

Royce was reviled by the proficiency involved to get clean kills. Ignorant shooters wasted extra shots to the buffalo's thick furred head, prolonging the damage before death, while educated sharpshooters shot through the less-dense ribs to pierce the lungs, often resulting in the beast falling instantly.

Royce Falco freed the strap over the revolver of his ammo-stocked gunbelt. His index finger curled expertly around where he would squeeze the trigger, the others taking to the grip, while his thumb rested on the hammer waiting to be cocked.

The Mustang 68; six-round single-action revolver with modified seven inch barrel, there'd be five cartridges of forty-four calibre ammunition chambered, all together bringing about three pounds or more of heft in hand.

Royce withdrew the Mustang, slowly, admiring the polished steel of the gun that had once been his choice of weapon until he was arrested...

Arrested...

But that wasn't until after this incident...

He had enough time to stop this slaughter all over again - the butchery of the buffalo, that is, not the carnage he'd bring upon the hunters.

Wherever Lafayette was, Royce would prove he was in the right during this confrontation.

Royce shot the weapon from the hip, fanning the hammer three times.

Three shooters nearby dropped.

Royce moved quickly to grab any revolvers he could lay his hands on. Five shots of his own would never be enough to take out an entire train's worth of hunters if he didn't get any time to reload.

But the three men never hit the floor...

Instead, their bodies faded from existence as they fell, their forms replaced by rising flames and shadows. The physical men had transformed into hellish spectres...

"What the fugg?" Royce breathed, a second passing before he moved again. "That is not how this day went down."

More of the hunters turned from their windows but were shot by Royce's quicker reactions. He fired his weapon plus another he'd procured but realised something was amiss.

He examined his old favourite. Royce hadn't realised that the chamber should have been empty until he'd fired around twice as many shots as possible. "More than five shots... what's going on?" He shrugged his shoulders and continued through the passenger cars.

Time didn't flow properly as the slaughter of the hunters repeated itself from that fateful day. There were moments when the wood walls of the train cars splintered around him as he returned fire that he'd be reliving the bloodshed that had continued to earn him the reputation of *Red Roy* as he remembered it, and other times when he'd suddenly be in another car or on the roof continuing the visceral mess.

The spirits of the recently deceased rose above the train and the buffalo, following the steam-billowing locomotive engine across the plains of Wakoda Territory. Ghostly horses emerged into existence under their new riders, galloping upon the sky above the bloodshed as though they could fly like eagles.

"They're not... are *they?*" Royce had to move on, ignoring memories of the myths of ethereal gallopers he had heard around the campfire of his Wakoda brother when he reached the front of the train. He stood over the coal in the tender, having maimed the pleading fireman with his own shovel, while explaining why what this train was doing was wrong.

He had the back of the engineer's head in the driver's cab lined within his revolver's custom sights, but slowly realised that he wasn't aiming at the rear of a sooty cap. Instead, it was the wide-brimmed midnight blue hat of Charles Lafayette.

"So here you are," Royce breathed, feeling lucky that he hadn't pulled the trigger on the magician.

The fireman begged for the engineer and his own lives, pleading that they were only doing their jobs, not harming any buffalo.

"Why, dear Royce," Lafayette slid around in the simple driver's seat at the boiler's backhead to face his would-be-attacker, "do you not kill the dog that unexpectedly turns upon the child?"

"What's that got to do with anything right now? You wanted to see me at my most justified!"

"This entire event has everything to do with you proving your justification. I reiterate; why do you favour the dog that turns upon the child?

"The dog doesn't know what it has done - it doesn't know any better."

"People are much the same, dear Royce. They must learn from their mistakes."

"This is completely different. And people should know better." The fireman continued to react as though his life was still being threatened.

"While mostly true," Lafayette motioned toward the fireman, "some can only know better when shown another way. They lived a life of never knowing, their mercy being that they must be taught."

"What," Royce tried to understand, "you think it's like teaching the dog that didn't know any better?"

"People can improve if shown another path. If offered mercy, a chance for redemption, they too can become the most loyal of companions. But, only if someone is there to guide them."

"People aren't like dogs."

"Royce Falco, their impending Doom is upon them at your own hands." The magician's voice came from behind and a pleading engineer was suddenly in the driver's seat – he was the very same train driver that had appeared as a ghost to Royce... a ghost that he had created on this day that had seen him sent to the gallows.

When he turned around, Lafayette was standing between the cab and the tender. "You have the power to weave their Fate along a different direction. A moment of Reckoning is upon you, do not waste the time Fate has allowed you..."

Cornelius wriggled in his pocket, a timely reminder about protective vigilance and what can occur when offering mercy to the living.

Royce didn't speak, but raised his revolver, the barrel pointing to the sky.

"Thus it shall be." Lafayette concluded.

"Yeah, yeah," Royce sighed, uncocking his revolver's hammer. "You *thus* and I'll *reckon*..."

The decisions of the outlaw Red Roy changed from this point onward. "You stop this train." Royce instructed the engineer instead of killing him, something he hadn't done the first time he'd been here. "And you refuse to drive it any further through buffalo territory, or ever drive a train for buffalo hunting again."

"Y-you got it, Mister." The engineer was almost tearing his cap apart in his nervous hands. "I got me a family in Sundown... you'll have made them so happy, a-and I'll only sign up for the passenger trains from now on. Promise."

"Me too," the fireman promised, holding his shovelled leg. "Got me a wife, children."

Royce was surprised more than he should have been by the men's words. The first time he was here, he'd never allowed them to tell – or perhaps he'd never allowed himself to hear – that they both had families...

Royce had taken these fathers away from their families, each departing this world by an unforgiving pull of the trigger and the merciless bullet that followed. "What had I become...?" They were families that would never know their fathers to be penitent men, better men upon their return if only Royce had chosen differently. Who was he to be their executioner of his own beliefs? "Why was a moment of reckoning rather than execution not something I'd ever dealt before?"

As the rift between the ways of Red Roy and Royce Falco widened, a church bell rang across the bloodied landscape: a death knell - tolled at the moment a person dies and their soul passes on.

It was dawn when Royce woke next. He'd managed to sleep through his Last Midnight – well, as far as he understood what had been happening to him.

Cornelius was still at his feet. After they take him to the gallows at 5 o'clock, Royce didn't know what would become of his rat friend.

Mortimer was back in his cell. Royce hadn't been disturbed by the old murderer's return. A penitentiary surgeon dressed wounds upon the wrinkled man with the unskilled assistance of McLaren and Reed.

No... this wasn't right, Royce thought... He had awoken to the sound of the clanging bell...

When the guards stood him up, Royce could see that Mortimer's bare chest and arms had been cut with strange lines that meant nothing to the ordinary observer. But Royce possessed some unwelcomed familiarity with such things.

The old man's rib cage and belly had been cut with three concentric circles that were crossed by three horizontal lines and three vertical lines, all as evenly spaced as a blade splitting flesh by hand would allow. Contrary to this symbol, though, whilst those lines were ritualistically perfect, the image was hacked by less precise cuts and gashes, spoiling the perfection of the Aetron symbol. Royce could see a pattern in the apparently random marks, the lines forming a bird of prey, if one were willing to see such a thing.

Mortimer's body was also traced with other cuts: bracelets of sliced flesh circled his wrists, monocles dug around each eye and a gash around the top of the skull as though he were to be scalped. Esoteric symbols etched in outwardly random places made no sense but to those that had carved them as art upon their living canvas.

What had the plague doctors done to Mortimer? To what purpose?

Royce's one non-Falco brother had whittled an Aetron symbol from wood to be a small pendant that hung from a leather necklace. He'd gifted his creation to him as a gift years before. The last time he had seen that brother, the man had fallen from the once spiritual grace he had lived by with the Wakoda. Royce didn't understand or experience Fate as his Wakoda brother had - perhaps a little fearful of such things due to his upbringing - but he gave the pendant back to its creator with the hopes that it may one day rekindle the spark of his sacred connection.

Mortimer cackled. "They cut me, Roy." He stood so the other prisoner could see better. Tears fell from his blood-circled eyes, but they were not tears of pain – they were tears of joy. "The plague doctors fugging cut me good. I could see myself in their covered eyes, like mirrors to my soul, their starving beaks and razor claws eager for my flesh." Tears mixed with the cuts around his recessed eyes, creating diluted scarlet puddles. "It was bliss as I waited for my turn... but then that big bell tolled again."

"What did I tell you about going on about that stupid bell?" Reed forced Mortimer to sit back down.

"You gotta admit," McLaren ignored Reed's reminder to the old man, "that's some spooky shyt with the ghost bell tolling a second time, like we're at some big cathedral funeral. Next up, I bet we'll see that black cat again!"

"Shut the fugg up, Mick!" Reed was incensed. "It was bad enough it set off all the prisoners in the rest of the Hole – you don't need to stir this one up any more than he already is about it."

"Did you hear it, Roy?" Mortimer tried, the pain of his tightened wounds being treated showing through his wincing voice.

"I did," Royce answered, "it woke me from... something..."

"You were sleeping like a baby, Falco," McLaren laughed. "You didn't wake up until we got this old codger back."

"Shut the fugg up. Everybody!" Reed was exasperated. "We don't need Mortimer being any more difficult."

"You don't understand!" Mortimer screamed. "I was going to have my turn on them, but that bell... that fugging bell!"

"It won't matter soon, old timer, it'll all be over for you." Reed was looking at the surgeon with a face that was commanding him to hurry the process along.

McLaren continued to steer the conversation on against Reed's wishes. "They said they had to do this to you, Mortimer, because you were infested with the diseased impulses of a murderer. Were they wrong?"

"Isn't hanging a man enough to stop him murdering?" Royce could see the plague doctors had really cut and beaten Mortimer, even parts of his face where the beard had been torn showed signs of brutalisation. The lunatic had been tortured. "Did they take their masks off; did you see any of them? Did they say anything?"

To what end? Some ritual? If Kayne was involved, Royce wondered why they didn't take him instead of Mortimer. Why not eliminate the only other contender from being the Seventh Son of a Seventh Son? Although, it didn't matter, the gallows would finish the job anyway...

"Con... Coo... Rah..." Mortimer didn't chuckle, but his eyes bulged with delight as a grin spread across his face, disrupting some of the wound dressings that the surgeon had administered.

"What, Mortimer?" Royce was up and holding the bars of his cell, facing the madman. "What did you say, what did *they* say?"

"The plague doctors... said he would come... Con-"

"Qonkura?" Royce saw Mortimer's head brighten further with recognition. "Did they say, Qo'n'ku'ra?"

McLaren and Reed looked at Royce with an odd regard, wondering what was just uttered, as Mortimer screamed, "He is coming, he comes forth, he is coming!" Reed hit the old man over the head with his wooden baton in response so the surgeon could finish his work.

McLaren came to Royce's cell. "Reed's right; don't stir him up, Falco. It's almost time to go. I suggest you use the bucket if you don't want it going everywhere when you hang."

"Thanks for that lovely picture in my head," Royce replied, countering with, "What's for breakfast?"

"You know you don't get fed before the execution… just emptied."

A priest entered the corridor of the cells. He was adorned in all manner of religious regalia and carrying a thick Bible with a prominent gilded crucifix on the cover.

Royce's mouth dropped: the priest was Charles Lafayette.

Royce wondered if appearing as other people - this time in the waking world - was a common occurrence for the magician.

McLaren nor Reed recognised the man that had performed card tricks for them the day before - or Clyde Mortimer, for that matter. It was just as it had been at the locomotive cab: only Royce recognised him. But there was no doubt in his mind that this finely-moustached clergyman was Charles Lafayette the magician.

Mortimer babbled at a rabid speed, going on about how he deserved a prayer, and how Red Roy wouldn't give him a pagan prayer, but perhaps he deserved a holy prayer instead, and that he should be spared the Void that the plague doctors had spoken of, and so forth, and on and on, until he was finally out of breath.

The surgeon was shown out by McLaren, having done as much as he could for Mortimer in the time remaining.

Reed said to the preacher, "You'll have to do whatever it is you're going to do on the way to the courtyard. These two have got to be hanging at the end of a noose by 5 o'clock."

III

The preacher - that to Royce was the exact likeness of Charles Lafayette - performed the Last Rites while walking to the gallows. Just like the magician, he spoke eloquently, but asked no questions and offered no sympathies for the pair to be executed. He never faltered, despite the continued ravings of Clyde Mortimer.

Irrespective of being led to his imminent death at the end of a rope, Royce was impressed by Lafayette's ability to maintain this charade by never making a visible regard to him at any moment. If it wasn't for knowing his face, the two would be complete strangers.

It was difficult to comprehend the Rites due to Mortimer's mad ranting and suddenly hearing Lafayette's noble accent enter his head. It was a bizarre experience, like having a conversation with your own mind.

Your Wakoda brother has passed your Aetron to one of his new allies, a young man from the East.

"...Hallowed be thy name..."

Those were the words that stuck with Royce the most, *Hallowed be thy name*, repeating in his head – much like *God be with you* had – along with the magician's dialogue. In moments he would be led to his death, apparently unable to be freed from this outcome by the esoteric tricks of a man that possessed mysterious powers Royce could never understand, or even be sprung by the apparently ever-present forgiving powers of the hallowed name being read about aloud that he understood even less.

"...For thine is the kingdom..."

This new ally is a nexus; where past, present, and future strands of Fate entwine.

"...And the power..."

This nexus does not yet understand his place within Mysterium, but your good brother does... but, so too will their enemies, the nexus shining like a beacon in the dark.

Enemies... The Law? Tycoons? The Army? Occultists? Royce hoped his brother hadn't done anything too stupid in his absence.

"...and the glory..."

Fate bound them together around the arrival of this nexus. They are without worldly guidance against the oncoming tide over the West. And I, I could not remain with them.

"...for ever..."

You left them?

Extend your protective vigilance to them, do more for people as well as beasts, become someone beyond what you believe possible.

A tear fell from Royce's face. But, I can't... I am going to die...

Did Red Roy not already die on that train waiting for his Last Midnight?

"...Amen..."

Fugg yeah, Amen to that...

Thus shall it be.

Just before entering the courtyard, McLaren bellowed, "It's that black cat again!"

Sure enough, Memphis crossed the path of the procession to the gallows, just before the open area where the reflective sheen remained from the previous night's passing storm.

And there it was...

The dawn's light of 5 o'clock was approaching and it shone upon the gallows, glistening against the soaked wood. There were two poles, both posts set with a hanging noose that waited inevitably for their victims.

The Warden was nearby, a bored look upon his face as he adjusted his monocle. Royce noticed a number of ravens on the rooves, lining long corridor edges and perched upon the sentry tower of the rear of Hayworth Penitentiary. Matters became grimmer as the three plague doctors arrived, their ominous presence unsettling the gathering.

The subsequent events were a blur for Royce, his mind racing as his time and his breath drew shorter than ever.

They were on the platform.

Mortimer had a black bag put over his head. The old man had become frantic. Breathing in and out rapidly, a wet circle dribbled at the mouth, real fear of his oncoming end manifesting. For the first time in his life, Clyde Mortimer was truly terrified... but offered no signs of repentance; it wasn't in his nature.

The last thing Royce saw as a bag was lowered over his eyes was a bunch of black birds and Charles Lafayette dressed like a priest.

Someone was reading aloud their crimes as ropes were placed around their necks, the nooses checked. The lists were extensive, and no sympathies were offered.

Warden Harry Linch observed the approaching hour upon his pocket watch as the executioner's hands went upon the lever that would remove the floor of the gallows beneath those sentenced to be hanged.

"It's 5 o'clock," the Warden told the executioner. "Necks must be broken!" With that simple command, the lever that held lives in balance was pulled and the floor gave way beneath the murderer Clyde Mortimer and outlaw Royce Falco.

As Royce fell to his Doom, uttering his last definitive words, "*Thus it shall be*," the mysterious church bell tolled again across Hayworth Penitentiary.

When the third bell tolled, panic ensued as two condemned men fell through a parted floor - but they would not hit the ground beneath due to the noose around their necks.

Every raven lined along the rooves and walls of Hayworth Penitentiary took flight when the bodies dropped and the bell rang, adding to the shock caused by the loud tolling while two people met their deaths.

A dread sensation shivered down the spines of many.

The plague doctors' beaked masks turned to each other, then the guards, anxious for answers.

"Hells fugging bells," McLaren called to the other guard, "that's a lych bell ringing!"

"Who cares, Mick." Reed didn't.

But McLaren did. "It's a corpse bell, tolled after someone dies."

After Reed continued to ignore him, McLaren inspected the hanging bodies while trying to block one ear, leaning to shake the rope around their necks. "This isn't Falco..."

Reed's face screwed up. "Whaddya mean?"

"It's a scarecrow!"

Reed couldn't believe his eyes, also seeing the straw stuffing coming from under Falco's hood. "Are you fugging kidding me?"

Mortimer was surely dead and hanged, but Royce Falco... gone... his body replaced by some farmyard effigy.

The preacher signalled back down the hallway toward the death-watch area from whence they had marched. "Gentlemen, I saw the outlaw Red Roy running back into the prison."

"It should be his ghost running back inside!" McLaren spat.

Twirling his moustache, the priest answered, "I wouldn't know of such things..."

As a much smaller gallows bell was rung, as an attempt to alert the prison of an escapee among the tolling church bell, the three plague doctors moved swiftly onto the gallows platform for what they had been waiting for.

The trio inspected the stuffed straw in the prison uniform that was topped with a burlap head - the dummy of Royce Falco a very unconvincing duplicate. They looked at each other through smoky lenses, then moved onto the single body that remained. The three produced tools from under their black robes with gloved hands. Blades, saws, hammers and chisels, among others – the instruments of surgeons.

The combined commotion of guards and bells caused more confusion than it helped among the overall heightening turmoil the entire prison was already under.

As the chaos spread, the plague doctors were left to dissect the lifeless remains of the murderous Clyde Mortimer as a manhunt for the escaped Royce Falco inside Hayworth Penitentiary had begun.

I

Royce Falco stumbled, suddenly aware that his feet were walking on solid ground. He winced as daylight struck his eyes, as though the executioner's bag was lifted from his head.

The intense tolling of the third haunting bell continued from Hayworth Penitentiary, a grim echo signalling that death had taken a soul.

He immediately clutched the noose that should have been at his neck, instead finding no rope or signs that he'd been hanged.

This wasn't one of Lafayette's weird dream trains, surely, because when he turned around his eyes followed the cobbled road leading all the way to the prison entrance. The old sign he'd observed when he first arrived still stood despite the storm, as it probably would continue to stand long after most of the prisoners had served their time or passed Beyond.

Royce released a dull, "Fugg." His first word after miraculously escaping the gallows. Shaking his head, he pondered the sign. "*Last Road into Hell*," he read out loud. That caused a quiet chuckle. "Well, apparently it's not..."

He felt a squirm in the pocket of ordinary everyday clothing – not the black and white striped uniform he'd become accustomed to - and brought forth his rat friend. The creature looked healthier than ever. "Did you have anything to do with this, Cornelius?"

The rat emitted a short chirp.

"I didn't think so, gotta be Laf-

"Sunnuvafugginbidge-horse!"

The sudden profanity was cussed alongside the snorting and squeal of a difficult horse, all followed by the sounds of crashing bodies.

Royce pocketed the rat. He quickly descended the outer rise of the valley that the prison was built in to find an angry rider already on his feet at the side of a road flogging his downed horse with a belt.

Blood boiling, Royce charged at the rider.

He caught the next whipping motion inside his hand. The intense shot of pain fuelled Royce's disarming of the makeshift weapon and his own subsequent returning strike with it.

The belt's rusty buckle smashed across the man's face, his hat flying. Blood spattered as his body flailed further from the road.

"What's this horse done to you?" Royce still held the belt, his fury crushing the leather strip.

The horse would have had a lush red chestnut coat if not for the obvious signs of cruelty and lack of care. Instead, the body was marred by excessive driving wounds and malnourishment caused the shape of ribs and other bones to be prominently evident. Flies blew around the wounds - Royce also aware that ravens circled above, waiting for the horse to become carrion.

"Fugg off! This's got nothing to do with you." The rider was back to his feet. "Stupid horse, he keeps giving up, bucking, doesn't obey."

"Because he can't," Royce turned back, "you've abused this animal," finding that the rider had a gun pointed at his face.

"Leave," the rider commanded, putting his hat back on, "or I'll put the horse's bullet in your face instead."

There was no hesitation. Royce had swung the belt up - a shot responding too late - hitting the revolver toward the sky. He lashed the belt at the rider, almost half of the end curling around the neck. He yanked him closer into a swinging curled fist.

As the rider toppled back to the ground, Royce caught the falling revolver and pointed it back at his face. What's your name?"

"Whadda you fugging care?"

"What's your fugging name?"

The rider hesitated until he heard Royce cock the weapon. "John... John Cassidy."

"Well, John, you should always click this here little hammer on your gun," Royce indicated where, as he aimed the weapon between the rider's eyes, "if you intend to shoot a man."

John pleaded, "Don't do it, mister, it's just a stupid horse!"

As Royce stared down the barrel to the rider's cowering face, gently squeezing the trigger that would end the cruel man's life, the horse stood up and forced a gentle whinny.

A reminder...

"You're lucky Red Roy died," the miraculous escapee tied the fearful man's arms to his side with the belt, "and Royce Falco lives."

"What? Red Roy's dead?"

Royce didn't answer the man that obviously didn't recognise him from wanted posters.

"John Cassidy tried another question. "What are you going to do to me?"

Royce took the horse's muddy head in both hands, noting the white striped blazes along the dirty pocked red coat, looking into his exhausted blue eyes. "You're going to be strong again, a champion." The horse's nostrils breathed small snorts upon the man and Royce responded by blowing gently back upon the nose.

"What are you doing?" John tried.

"Shaking hands..." Royce smiled at the horse. "What's his name?"

"I never named the stupid thing."

"Every soul deserves a name." Royce looked intently into the animal's eyes. "We'll find out your name, together, hey?"

"What are you going to do to me?"

"Be thankful I didn't kill you." Royce took a lasso from the horse's saddle and reworked it to tether John, hands bound, along behind the horse. "Your Fate lies along a different path." He then took the hat from John's head, placing it upon his own.

"Hey, that's my hat!"

"You don't deserve such a fine hat." Royce adjusted the brim of the bowler hat between two fingers upon his head. "And you won't need it while you're following the horse, learning some manners."

Royce placed his rat companion on the horse's saddle. "Watch this piece of shyt, Cornelius, will you?"

"What are you doing with that stinking rat?"

"He gets to ride the horse, not you."

"But it's my fugging horse!"

"You also don't deserve such a noble creature. This horse can't take a rider, for now, because of how you've treated him."

"Let me fugging go!"

Royce ignored the command, checking inside the saddlebags. "You've got oats and water, and your horse is starving to death?"

"So what? He's useless."

"You're useless..." Royce fed the famished animal by hand and cupped water to its dry thirsty mouth for it to drink. His thoughts dwelled upon the events leading up his miraculous escape of the gallows. Charles Lafayette had probably made his last appearance now that the ordeal was over, like a performer exiting the stage after a show. "But you could be better. And this horse will become a champion."

"Where are we going?"

"To find my Wakoda brother."

John was confused. "You have an Indian brother?"

With no answer, the Hayworth Penitentiary escapee took the reins of the horse and led him slowly onward with the tethered captive trudging behind.

Royce Falco left the haunted prison of mysterious tolling bells behind, but would take the dread reckoning of his Last Midnight wherever he may roam.

HORSE NATION

Matteo and Nickolas Tobin have spent years using their career as surveyors to fund their side project of investigating supernatural phenomena across the Wild West.

A native Wakoda ritual that the brothers stumble upon while exploring the area of Otter Creek will change them forever when they discover that the forces of Fate had destined them to be participants in the ceremony.

Whether Matteo and Nickolas will accept their role in that destiny is another matter.

GHOST RIDERS

The Civil War is over. American expansion pushes westward across the United States, unaware of the supernatural dangers that lurk in the Wild West.

A Bostonian tourist is thrust against his will into this savage land of outlaws and desperados. Finding allies in a war veteran, a native tracker, a gold rush baroness, a mysterious magician and a trusty dog, Jacobi Nicholson will find that he is destined to heal some of the scars this unforgiving landscape has given his new friends.

Bound by the spectres of an old frontier myth, will the gang defy the Law to do what is right and go beyond legend...?

BROKEN WINGS

Erica's father wasn't aware of the terrifying monster that lurked below their ranch in the abandoned gold mine.

If he had known, he may not have announced that he was going to build a Flying Machine by the Fourth of July. He may not have worked on the contraption with such a manic fever, oblivious of his dying wife. And, he may have been able to avoid the monster feeding on what was left of his fragile mind.

For Erica's father, the Flying Machine and his quest for the sky had to succeed - nothing else mattered!

DREAD RECKONING

Royce Falco is scheduled for execution in the Hayworth Penitentiary.

His usual confidence to slip from such situations is crushed when a mysterious visitor brings news that his demise has been orchestrated, but also brings an offer to alter his fate... the decision will come at a price.

Dread sets in as Royce's last midnight approaches in the reputably haunted prison, because at 5 o'clock they take him to the gallows post.

SILENT ECHOES

An entire train and its passengers have mysteriously vanished from Echo Station overnight without a trace.

The only clues to solving the impossible occurence arrive in the form of a series of increasingly frantic messages that were telegraphed to the town of Sundown during the night of the vanishing. Descriptions abound of sinister men in beaked masks and heavy cloaks that the sender names as plague doctors, and monsters that remain unnamed.

With only the raving telegraphs as evidence, this may be an investigation that can't be solved.

www.ingramcontent.com/pod-product-compliance
Lightning Source LLC
Chambersburg PA
CBHW021704110726
47902CB00007B/2056